SWIM
a story of feeling

Joshua Bulpin

Thanks

To people I have worked with in challenging environments over the years who have taught and continue to teach me so much about the human experience, both shiny and shit.

To those I love. I love you. Let the learning on this oft ridiculous journey continue.

Libby

*One day
you finally knew
what you had to do, and began,
though the voices around you
kept shouting
their bad advice*

*

*as you strode deeper and deeper
into the world,
determined to do
the only thing you could do –
determined to save
the only life that you could save.*

Mary Oliver

TREADING WATER

There they were, the Person, treading water in the ocean. As were a few others, treading water around them.

The treading of the water was committed, and in various styles. If anyone were to observe their efforts, they would have seen that to all intents and purposes each individual was an expert at keeping themselves afloat.

Every now and then, when the sea turned into white horses, and the wind got up or one of the group got tired, one of them would, without thought or intention, grab hold of the nearest other to stay afloat. Only when the other was almost drowned themselves did they let go.

Swimmers sporadically passed by the expert floaters on their way to shore. They would stop, tread water with the group for a while and then swim on, headed for land.

Sometimes these swimmers suggested a member of the group swim to land with them. These swimmers told the Person that further in-shore there was some shelter, there was even more on land, and if they swam to that shelter they could safely ride-out the storm, then swim back out to the ocean any time they wanted. the Person was tempted, they all were, but none of them knew how to swim, only how to tread water.

When the Swimmers visited the Person would offer great advice on how to tread water well, but would not listen to those that encouraged them to learn to swim. So they stayed where they were. Furiously treading water to stay afloat, occasionally being grabbed by others in their desperation, and in turn sometimes holding onto others in theirs.

Presently a couple of the other people began to listen to the swimmers. They tried to have a little swim. They swam for a while, not very well, and after not getting very far would give up and again take-up their furious, confident and assured treading water. No swimming for them thank you.

The Person was curious about the land. The group of people, having never been there were adamant it wasn't all that and so they focused on perfecting treading water, and advising swimmers who dropped by on how to improve their technique.

As the Swimmers continued to visit the Person began to listen to what they were saying about swimming, about land, and about something else - sailing on boats. The Person had seen a few boats in the ocean, they had even climbed aboard one once or twice. Once the Person had slipped off the top rope of the boarding ladder, and another time the Person jumped overboard when a storm approached. The group agreed that the best way to avoid being on a boat in a storm was not to get on board a boat at all. Not when they could tread water so well.

The Swimmers told the Person that with swimming and boating storms are easier, and that they can always come back to treading water, alone or with the other people, whenever they want.

The Person was befuddled and began to shout at others in the group, telling them they were wrong to only tread water.

They Person however continued treading water, teaching others when they dropped in during their swim.

Use whatever knowledge you have but understand its limitations.
Knowledge alone isn't enough, it has no heart.
No amount of knowledge will ever nourish or sustain your spirit.
It cannot bring happiness or peace.
Life requires intense feeling and constant energy.
Life demands right action if knowledge is to come alive.

Dan Millman

THE BOAT

Out of the mist appeared a Boat. It was a leaky Boat with tattered sails and a motor low on fuel, but it worked. It was the most beautiful Boat the Person had ever seen.

The Boat approached the Person and offered them a ride to shore. In return all the Boat asked was for the Person to help bail out the water every now and then.

The Boat trusted the Person. The Person couldn't believe their luck, and after forgetting all their previous concerns, climbed aboard.

Once aboard the Person was bitten by a grumpy little Crab. Suddenly the Person remembered their fear of being in the Boat. Only now they added the thought that the Crab might bite them again.

They jumped back into the sea, began treading water furiously and pushed the Boat away.

The Boat didn't leave. It kept re-assuring the Person that although a little leaky it was sound and if they hurried up there was still enough fuel left for them to make it to land, ride out the approaching storm and leave the Crab on a rock.

The Person was desperately tempted but too afraid. The Person would not get back on board, but asked the Boat to stay close as the storm on the horizon grew ever closer.

In time the Boat told the Person the leaks were getting worse and the fuel was running out. It needed to go back to shore or it would sink. The Person heard the Boat and continued to tread water, and so it headed back to shore alone.

After the Boat had gone the Person considered what they had and hadn't thought and done. For a while they blamed the Boat for turning up with a Crab on board.

As the storm approached the Person trod water ever more furiously and looked around for something or someone to keep them afloat.

*When we are comfortable and inattentive,
we run the risk of committing grave injustices
absentmindedly*

Chinua Achebe

THE SEABIRD

A Sea Bird landed close to the Person. It told them they had seen the Boat arrive safely if a little worse for wear after a tough journey back to shore.

The Sea Bird asked the Person if they were ready to swim. It gave the Person a few lessons based on what they had seen others doing.

As the Sea Bird offered encouragement, working hard to ride the thermals and conserve their own energy for the journey back to nest, the sun came out.

The Person began to swim. They swam hard and with little grace. Sometimes they went round in circles, and wound up treading water again, trying to work out which way to go, and how.

The Person shouted at the Sea Bird for not directing them properly.

After some time the Sea Bird was exhausted. The Sea Bird offered one last burst of encouragement, and flew off to feed its' little ones back in the nest.

I am a human being. Nothing human can be alien to me.

Terence

THE PERSON

The Person was alone again. Others in the group continued to tread water, doing their own thing. Some were learning to swim, and some were talking with boats.

The Person contemplated what might happen when the next storm arrived.

Swimmers continued to pass by, stopping to tread water, taking tips from the Person and offering their own advice in turn. The Sea Bird flew over often shouting a hello, silently hoping. There was no sign of the Boat.

With all the Person now knew and didn't know, and with all they felt; there was a choice to be made.

Stay there, treading water brilliantly. Or begin to swim.

*The true value
of life
is not measured
by what we leave behind,
but how fiercely we love
and are loved in return
while we're here*

Beau Taplin

The ability to feel with integrity, to be honestly human and to use those feelings healthily is a gift we can give others.

First we must give it to ourselves.

Say hello at www.thejoshuatrails.com

Printed in Poland
by Amazon Fulfillment
Poland Sp. z o.o., Wrocław